CRT

TITCHY WITCH

AND THE BABYSITTING SPELL

For Sylvie
R.I.

For Fred with lots of love
K.M.

ORCHARD BOOKS
338 Euston Road
London NW1 3BH
Orchard Books Australia
Level 17/207 Kent Street, Sydney, NSW 2000

First published in Great Britain in 2013
First paperback publication 2014
ISBN 978 1 40830 716 8 (HB)
ISBN 978 1 40830 720 5 (PB)

1 3 5 7 9 10 8 6 4 2 (HB)
1 3 5 7 9 10 8 6 4 2 (PB)
Printed in China

Orchard Books is a division of Hachette Children's Books, an Hachette UK company.
www.hachette.co.uk

TITCHY WITCH

AND THE BABYSITTING SPELL

BY ROSE IMPEY   ILLUSTRATED BY KATHARINE McEWEN

ORCHARD

Titchy-witch was in a *very* bad mood. Mum and Dad were getting ready to go out — without *her*!

They were off to a witches' and
wizards' spell-sharing party.
It was the first time they had
been out alone together since
Weeny-witch was born.

Titchy-witch wanted to go too.
But she had to stay at home with
Cat-a-bogus, who was far too bossy
for her liking!

Cat-a-bogus wasn't exactly looking
forward to little-witch-sitting either.
Weeny-witch was no trouble at all
— she would soon be fast asleep.

But Titchy-witch was wide awake,
and trouble was her middle name.

Titchy-witch had to find a way to
keep Mum and Dad at home.
First she hid Mum's hat up the
chimney.

Then she dropped Dad's shoes
down the toilet!

Finally, she gave the baby
chicken pox all over.

When none of these things worked, Titchy-witch pretended to have a tummy ache.

So Cat-a-bogus brought out
his special medicine. It tasted
disgusting!

Poo! Yuk! No, thanks!

Magically, Titchy-witch's
tummy ache seemed to disappear.

At last it was time to wave Mum
and Dad goodbye.

"Be a good little witch till we get
home!" they told her.
Cat-a-bogus didn't think that was
very likely.

Even when he made Titchy-witch's favourite supper, beetleburgers with bats' blood ketchup, Titchy-witch refused to eat it.

She went off to her room in a *bad*
mood.

"I know what I need," she told Dido.

"A bring-Mum-and-Dad-home spell!
This will be a diddle-doddle."

Uh oh!

Broomstick malfunction, lost keys and hats,
Freak storms and swarms of vampire bats.
Spots, bumps and itches, aches, bites and pains,
Bring Mum and Dad back home again!

It sounded like a pretty angry spell
– and a scary one!
It was so scary that Titchy-witch
rushed to lock it in the cupboard.

But little bits of it escaped
and flew out of the window.

Titchy-witch went and hid under
her bed.

But the spell was rattling the
cupboard door trying to get out.
She ran downstairs to escape from it.

Titchy-witch begged Cat-a-bogus
to play endless games
of Disappearing Dragons
and Exploding Snap with her.

And even after that she *still* didn't want to go to bed!
She was thinking of that scary spell rattling her cupboard door.

Soon it was so late Titchy-witch
couldn't keep her little eyes open
any more.

So Cat-a-bogus carried her up to bed.

Suddenly, Titchy-witch was wide awake again, asking for one last haunty story, an extra cup of unicorn's milk and yet another wee!

Cat-a-bogus knew *something* was
wrong. The cat came and sat on
her bed.

"What's *really* going on?" he asked
Titchy-witch.

Titchy-witch pointed to the
cupboard doors.

When Cat-a-bogus looked inside,
he shook his head.
He wondered when this little witch
would ever learn *not to meddle
with magic.*

The cat soon got rid of that scary
spell with a few magic words of his
own:

Hocus pocus, alakazam!
Hop it, spell!
Be gone! Go! Scram!

Then he made a special sweet
dreams spell, full of Titchy-witch's
favourite things.
In fact, everything a little witch
could ever wish for:

Surprise presents, cuddles with Dido, doing swirlies on her broomstick and lots and *lots* of chocolate grobblies.

Just as Titchy-witch was drifting off to sleep, Mum and Dad arrived home early.
They'd had a bit of trouble with the broomstick and a few pesky bats!

"Anyway, we were missing you and Weeny-witch too much," said Mum, giving her a kiss.

Titchy-witch went off to sleep a very happy little witch.

TITCHY WITCH

BY ROSE IMPEY ILLUSTRATED BY KATHARINE McEWEN

Enjoy a little more magic with all the Titchy-witch tales:

Orchard Books are available from all good
bookshops, or can be ordered from our website:
www.orchardbooks.co.uk
or telephone 01235 827702, or fax 01235 827703.

Prices and availability are subject to change.